# THE
# CHEETAH-GIRL

*(Being the manuscript not published with the collection under the title of "The Purple Saphire".)*


DEPOSITED BY
THE PROFESSOR OF PHYSIOLOGY
IN THE UNIVERSITY OF COSMOPOLI

THIS IS A SNUGGLY BOOK

The current edition is a the same text which was originally printed in 1923 in an edition of 20 copies.

ISBN: 978-1-64525-130-9

# THE CHEETAH-GIRL

Edward Heron-Allen (1861-1943) was an English polymath, writer, scientist and scholar. Writing under a number of pseudonyms, as well as his own name, his works cover numerous forms of literature and fields, including those of Persian poetry, violins, chiromancy, and foraminifera, though he is probably best remembered today for his forays into fantastic fiction under the pseudonym of Christopher Blayre. His publications include *Chiromancy, or the science of palmistry* (1883), *Violin-Making, as it was and is* (1884), the volume of poetry *The Love-Letters of a Vagabond* (1889), a translation from the Persian of *The Lament of Bābā Tāhir* (1902), *Barnacles in Nature and in Myth* (1928), *The Cheetah-Girl* (1923), *The Strange Papers of Dr. Blayre* (1932), and *Asparagus as a Hobby for Amateurs* (1934).

SNUGGLY BOOKS

# NOTE OF EXPLANATION.

THE note by my Publishers on page 211 requires an explanation which circumstances rendered it both difficult and desirable to offer in that place. The seven published MSS. were selected by me from among a large number of which I had become custodian, as explained in my Ante-script to "The Purple Sapphire" and at the same time I brought away with me from the safe in the University library, for re-perusal, the MS. of "*The Cheetah-Girl.*" This MS., though setting forth the principles of an enquiry, and experiments, in a branch of Biological research the importance of which it would be impossible to over-estimate, contains matters of record of such a nature that it could not possibly be published in a volume destined for public circulation. The table of contents was, however, compiled from the Title covers of the MSS. by my Secretary, who, I may mention parenthetically, made the mistake of writing "Deposited by the Professor of Biology" instead of "Of Physiology"—there is no chair of general Biology in the University of Cosmopoli. This "table" went to the Printers after my departure from England on a protracted holiday, and was "set-up" with

7

the rest of what is technically called "the preliminary matter". When, on my return, my Publishers asked for this MS. I considered that I was justified in showing it to them in confidence, and they at once agreed with me that it could not be printed. Hence the "Note" which Reviewers have regarded, some in the light of a joke (!), and some as a touch of intentional sensationalism.

CHRISTOPHER BLAYRE.

# THE
# CHEETAH-GIRL

# THE CHEETAH-GIRL.

I have spent a long and very tiring day in London, and I have come home, worn out physically and mentally. But I have settled all my worldly affairs, and am, I think, prepared for any eventuality. I am now ready therefore to kill my wife on the first opportunity that offers.

I have written that deliberately; so as to see and to realise how terrible it looks, written down to "stiffen myself" so to speak, for, if it be possible, I admire my wife even more to-day than I did when we set out upon our wonderful honeymoon, just over three months ago. But, terrible as it is to contemplate, she must die as soon as possible; the welfare of the Race demands her death. There is bound to be an inquest, and I dread, even now, what the Post-mortem examination of her beautiful body may reveal. The manner of her death I have thought out and decided upon, and there is not, I believe, the slightest possibility of my being connected in the remotest degree with the tragedy, but I have deemed it expedient to make such arrangements as regards my affairs as may become necessary in the event of my being hung for murder. For I should not offer any defence or explanation of my act—I owe that to her, to her mother, to my predecessor in the chair of Physiology in the University, and to the memory of three months of the most passionate happiness which have ever fallen to the lot of man. And even if I did explain my action, would my explanation be believed? Perhaps it might, in the light of proofs I could bring forward, but would life be possible for me among human beings afterwards? A thousand times *No*. But I owe it to Science to record the circumstances which have led to the step I am henceforth seeking the opportunity to take. I shall deposit this record with the Registrar of the University, with precautions that it shall not be read until many years have elapsed after my death—I have no near relations, and I shall not marry again—therefore no one living can be hurt. And in any case the facts I have to record, whilst of paramount importance to Physiologists in the future, can never be given any wide publicity—if indeed they can be imparted to anyone at all, excepting under the seal of professional secrecy.

Thus much by way of introduction. My record must commence with the year 19—, when, having taken my degrees of Doctor of Medicine had Doctor of Science, I was appointed Assistant and Demonstrator to Professor Paul Barrowdale, F.R.S., Professor of Psychology in the University of Cosmopoli. With our academic duties I am not concerned now, and the records, so far as they could be published, of the research work done in the laboratory of that daring and brilliant Physiologist are to be found scattered among pages of the contemporary journals of Science. It is with our personal relations that I am constrained to deal. These became, almost from their inception, of the most intimate nature; in our work in the University, I recognised in him a brilliant master; he recognised in me a devoted and assiduous pupil; outside our professional connection our tastes, our views, were strangely identical. He was no narrow-minded or ascetic Scientist, and, away from the University, his appreciation of the pleasures of life, of "wine, woman and song," of travel, literature and art found a ready response in me, and we became confidential friends and companions, to a degree which is very rare between a Professor and his Assistant.

There was only one subject upon which he never touched even in our moments of closest intimacy and confidence and in regard to which I never attempted to break the seal of silence which he had imposed upon himself, and tacitly upon me. This subject was Mrs. Clayton. As regards this lady, though the gossip which is indigenous to a University town no doubt from time to time formulated theories (for Barrowdale was a very free-living bachelor, was, as such, looked askant upon by many of the Professorial Staff and their wives) no one would ever "come out into the open," so to speak, for the all-sufficient reason that any scandal openly promulgated would have to be rapidly sterilised, should Barrowdale have shown any signs of wanting to marry any daughter of the University, and much will be tacitly ignored in a bachelor professor of more than ample private means.

Mrs. Clayton lived in a charming little house about three miles out of the town. It was understood that Barrowdale was her trustee and had charge of her busi-ness-affairs. There was a child, a girl, whom no one ever saw, but whether the child was born after Mrs. Clayton's arrival in the neighbourhood, or before that event, no one was in a position to say. One Academic lady (with daughters) had gone so far as to ascertain that the child, whose curious name was "Uniqua," was not registered at birth in the District Registry. Beyond this nothing was known; Barrowdale never afforded any intelligence, and if, as was whispered from time to time with bated breath, "*à quatres yeux*" she was his daughter, there was nothing on record to convey the slightest indication or *a priori* evidence of the fact.

I saw her once—I was walking with Barrowdale and we met Mrs. Clayton and the child, an ugly, sallow, swarthy little thing, who struck me as singularly repellent and uninteresting. Mrs. Clayton was a nervous, faded person, gentle in manner and appearance, but quite unnoticeable. She went nowhere and knew no one. Neither mother nor daughter interested me in the least. Now and then I believe an undergraduate would refer contemptuously to "old Barrowdale's woman," but there was no "talk," in the Unversity sense of the word. Several years passed by during which our work in the Laboratory and Schools, and our pleasures in companionship, grew more and more intimately connected, so much so that I refused the offer of a Professorship in a Northern University rather than be separated from Barrowdale—for the work we were engaged upon was of the highest Physiological importance. He was grateful to me for this, and I know that he never lost an opportunity of impressing upon the Authorities that I was his natural and indicated successor in the Chair of Physiology on his death or retirement. This came about

14

one day with appalling suddenness. Barrowdale had been seedy, nervy "off colour," for several days. He had been out more than once to see Mrs. Clayton, as I knew, and one evening came home tired to death and drenched to the skin. The next day he was in a high fever, in the evening sceptic pneumonia of a most virulent type set in, and in twenty-four hours he was dead.

I found that he had made me, together with his solicitor, a worthy old man in London, his Executor and Trustee. He provided an annuity of £600 a year for Mrs. Clayton, which on her death devolved to Uniqua. The rest of his property, he being apparently alone in the world, was bequeathed to the University. The good woman, who seemed absolutely paralysed by the death of Barrowdale, came into Cosmopoli to see me whenever her affairs required an interview, always the same nervous uninteresting creature. I confess I hoped she would be led on some occasion to speak of Uniqua's father, but in spite of one or two "leads" she never "followed," and, being really quite uninterested in the matter, I never tried to press the subject.

In due course, almost mechanically, I succeeded Barrowdale in the chair of Physiology, and I had neither time nor inclination to concern myself about my two "*cestuis que trustent.*"

We come then by effluxion of time to the end of last term. The men were due to go down for the Long Vacation next day, and I had made all arrangements for a protracted tour down the Loire and through the Midi of France. I may mention that Barrowdale left me by his will the comfortable and comforting legacy of £10,000.

Some paper came to me on this memorable day from my co-trustee, connected with a change of investment, which required Mrs. Clayton's signature. There was no time to communicate by post, so I jumped into my two-seater and ran out to her house. I rang the bell and the door was opened by the most Beautiful Being that I had ever seen in my life—and I had seen a good many.

"Mrs. Clayton—?" I began.

"Mother is out," she replied, "you are Professor Magley? Please come in."

She held out her hand, which I took, and without letting go of mine, she drew me into their sitting-room, a cosy little place furnished with great taste (Barrowdale's taste) and strewn with fur rugs which gave off a warm sensuous perfume. The touch of the girl's hand was electrical, it sent a thrill of intense desire up my arm to my brain, and when she dropped my hand and stood before me, her lips parted in a smile more provoking than anything of the kind I had ever seen, I was simply struck dumb, and stood looking at her, my heart beating violently.

She was a lithe creature of rather more than average stature, draped, rather than dressed, in a kind of dull red silk wrapper, confined at the waist by a suede leather belt. It folded across her breasts (one of which, perfect in form, almost escaped from the folds) and came down to just below her knees—her legs were bare, and her feet were shod in fur-lined slippers. I verily believe that, save for this garment, she was naked. Her face was indescribable, a mass of purple-black hair gathered into a loose bunch on the top of her head, thick dark eyebrows shadowing long lazy eyes which seemed to me to be enormous, her complexion a tawny russet brown, with a suspicion of down on the cheeks and more than a suspicion of it at the corners of her upper lip. She had let her hands fall by her sides, and as she looked at me with that marvellous smile, the tip of a crimson tongue passed slowly across her lower lip from one side to the other. I was struck, even at that wonderful moment, by the comparative prominence of her little canine teeth, which gave an indescribable and characteristic charm to her smile.

Without saying a word, and, I declare, without any conscious volition of my own, I held out my arms, and she stepped forward into them. I crushed her body to me and our lips joined. I thought until then that I knew what it was to be kissed. I did not. The lingering passion of Uniqua's kiss was unlike anything I had ever dreamed of as possible. Her tongue which sought mine was strangely long and firm, and even in the delirium of the moment it seemed to me that her lingual papillae were accentuated almost to the point of roughness, but the exquisite power of it defies words. Her arms were round me, her legs were twisted into mine, and I think I should have fallen had she not gently disengaged herself and, still holding me by one arm she drew me towards a low divan covered with fine skins from which I had evidently aroused her. As she reached it she flung herself down upon the skins, and as she fell one beautifully modelled leg, bare to mid-thigh, escaped from the folds of her wrapper. She raised her arms to me in a gesture of divine invitation—and at that moment the door opened and Mrs. Clayton came in.

I do not know what was to be read from my face as I turned towards her, but if it was a reflection of Uniqua's,

Mrs. Clayton must have been blind indeed if she did not take in the situation at a glance. I began, very haltingly, to utter apologies and to explain my visit. She was obviously very much upset and distressed, but all she said was—in short, disjointed sentences:—

"I see, I see. I could not have expected—no one comes here—I should not have gone out—I never do. Please bring the papers in here"—and she led me into the dining room, where there were pens and so on.

All this time Uniqua had not moved or uttered a sound, but just lay curled up luxuriously on the divan, watching me with her huge eyes, and, as it were, "swaying" her beautiful smile from side to side—I cannot describe it otherwise. The slipper had fallen from the foot of the leg which still lay unconcernedly outside her "sarong," and here was the only movement that she made. The toes opened and shut and curled inwards towards the palm of her foot with a regulated movement which seemed to me to be indicative of extreme and perfect luxury.

Mrs. Clayton signed the papers, with a shaky hand it is true, but said nothing about Uniqua. The silence becoming oppressive, I thought it obvious and tactful to say:—

"Your daughter has grown into a very striking young woman."

"Yes—very," replied the poor woman nervously, "very. I never leave her if I can help it—but expecting no one, I went in next door for something—the servant is out—and so," she tailed off incoherently, and I saw that I was distressing her, so I took my leave as casually as I could, with my blood boiling in my veins and my heart throbbing.

When I got outside I took a deep breath, but I seemed saturated with the tense, sensuous perfume of Uniqua's room and of Uniqua herself, for, whether it was contact with her divan or what, her whole body gave off a perfume for which there was only one word—it was intoxicating—slightly savage. It clung to me all the way back to my rooms, and even afterwards when I had opened all the windows. I need hardly say that I could not get her out of my thoughts all day—nor did I want to—and I dreamed a dream!

Next morning, as I went on with my packing, and the College was rapidly emptying of the men off on Long Vacation, I said to myself:—

"Look here, my son, you are that girl's guardian. Barrowdale has entrusted her to you. It's a damned good thing that you are off to-morrow for three months—and when you get back again, keep clear of it"—Thus I apostrophized myself, and I knew that I wanted Uniqua more than anything else in the world.

By the afternoon the College was practically empty, and I had finished my packing, and was trying to read an abstruse German treatise on Cytology—but I couldn't. My senses were on edge—unnaturally keen—hypertrophied as it were. I heard a step in the Quad, it "slithered" up my stair—a rap on the door—I knew who it was before the door was flung open. In an instant we were in one another's arms. The long witchery of her kiss, the invitation of her magical tongue, everything was my dream come true. I had in my rooms a divan no less vivid with willing complicity than the one at the cottage; we fell upon it without a word, and in spite of the fact that Uniqua was in a physical condition in which it is customary for young women to withhold themselves from active caress, we gave ourselves up to one another, naturally, unthinkingly, in a whirl-wind orgy of exquisite possession and ecstasy.

Presently, when we were able to talk—for until then not a word had been uttered on either side—I asked her how she had got away.

"Mother's had a sleepless night," she said, "and this afternoon she locked the front and back doors and went to bed. I got out of the window. I wanted you so frightfully."

An hour passed in a delirium of sensuous delight which cannot be hinted at—not from motives of reticence, for I am determined to record here the absolute facts as they occurred, without any periphrasis, but because the marvel that was Uniqua simply beggars and defies description. I thought I had known passion—fool! I had never even touched its fringe.

If Uniqua was wonderful to behold in her dull red sarong, what was she naked! No painter or sculptor ever imagined, much less reproduced, so perfect a body; her beautiful breasts stood out in perfect proportion, the nipples prominent and surrounded with a silky aureole of tiny purple curls, tender and fascinating. Her axillary hair was phenomenally thick and I speedily found that to be kissed and petted under her arms drove her frantic with delight. I have had reason to remember and be thankful for this, as will be seen later. The whole of her body was covered with the light soft down such as is seen upon many fair women, but upon Uniqua it was deeper in shade than usual, and it was punctuated here and there with little streaks, and sometimes almost circles of a still deeper tone. From her navel downwards it increased into a glorious mass of pubic hair which extended from hip to hip, and though so dense, was of the most amazingly soft texture, covering the Whole of the lower stomach and intercrural space with a veritable "*fourrure*"—it was wonderful, and, to repeat the only adjective which describes any of Uniqua's esoteric attributes—intoxicating. Her forearms and legs were deliciously hirsute, and even up and down her spine a narrow furry band invited one's most ingenious caresses. Whoever gave her the name of Uniqua knew what he was about—prophetically.

We were lying in one another's arms, whispering passionate secrets to one another, I in a silk bath-robe, and she clad only in her wonderful skin and hair, when the door—which we had never thought of locking—was flung open, and Mrs. Clayton stood before us—frankly petrified and aghast.

I sprang to my feet and burst into words:

"Do not misjudge us," I cried, "we love one another as I never dreamed it possible to love. We shall be married at once—I will get a licence to-morrow, and next day Uniqua will be my wife. Forgive us the passion that has made us irresistible to one another—you will understand, I am sure—you are a woman who has loved, and you are her mother. Now you will have a devoted son as well as a daughter."

I paused. Mrs. Clayton had not said a word, she had fallen into a chair and, ashy-white, looked back and forth from me to Uniqua, who, utterly unconscious of her exquisite nakedness, lay on the divan, looking at us—with the same wonderful smile that had overwhelmed and held me, her crimson tongue passing to and fro across her lower lip. Then Mrs. Clayton got up—apparently with an effort—and she said:—

"No—no—*no*. It cannot, it can never be. You don't know. Oh! I am a wicked woman! At these times she is not responsible for what she does—and besides, she knows nothing. I never let her out of my sight until the time—the danger is over. Let me take her away!"

"But my dear lady," I said, "reflect a moment. We *must* be married now. We are both—I comparatively—young, and for a University Professor I am rich. I will be the best of husbands to her—the best of sons to you. Our old friend Barrowdale would have wished it, I am sure. I was his favourite—his only intimate friend."

At Barrowdale's name the poor woman started as if she had been stung.

"No, no, no," she cried again, "he would not—he would have killed himself and her rather. It has all been so sudden—I have not had time—forgive me for God's sake, and let me take her away."

"Well then, let us be engaged for a short while," I said ineptly.

"No, never. She must never marry. She can't. Oh, don't torture me!"

There was no reasoning with her. She was like a mad woman. Uniqua stood up in all her glorious statuesque nudity and allowed her mother to dress her with shaking hands whilst I looked on. I cut a poor figure. When she was dressed Mrs. Clayton took her away. She went without casting a look in my direction.

I was simply stunned.

I can give no description of the phantasmagoria of my thoughts for the rest of the afternoon and evening. One thing was certain: I could not leave England without having this matter cleared up and placed upon a proper, the only possible, basis. I thought and thought. What mad idea could the woman have? I tried to reason it out—I racked my brains for an explanation but found none. The girl was alive with passion, she was predestined to fall into the hands of some casual sensualist—what better solution, if her passion was in part, or in any way, pathological, than to give her to a husband who would look after her? I wearied myself with thoughts, and tumbled into bed at midnight.

At 3 a.m. I was awakened by a rapping at my door. I started into vivid wakefulness—It could only be Uniqua. It was. I subsequently learned that she had got past the Porter with a statement that her mother had sent her with a message of vital urgency—and with other inducement.

"I have got away again, sweet lover of mine," she said, as I took her in my arms. "Mother is mad, I think. Hide me—and take me away with you. Marry me or not, I don't care, I love you and want you so frightfully that I could kill anyone who stood between us."

What was I to do? I wanted her just as badly as she wanted me. She wanted to be loved—had, there and then—but I, with that practical good sense which I flatter myself distinguishes me, made coffee and toast and an omelette, and made her eat with me. Then we stole down and got past the heavily bribed Porter (remember Term was over, and he was once more a human being, and I no longer a Professor) reached the garage, carrying my bags which were already packed, got out the car and made a bee-line for London, where we put up at a quiet west-central hotel. Next day, I visited my co-trustee early, whilst Uniqua went shopping. She had of course come away wholly unprovided with any sort of *trousseau*. I confided the facts, in outline, to my co-trustee (who was horribly shocked!) got a Special Licence at Doctor's Commons, and in the shortest possible time we were married at a Registry and fled—yes, we absolutely fled— to Paris. From Paris we both wrote to Mrs. Clayton announcing the inevitable, irredeemable event, but we gave her no address, merely saying that we should be away for at least three months, and would send an address for her to write to and forgive us. The only person to whom I confided my whereabouts was the horrified lawyer.

I could, in normal circumstances, take a vivid pleasure in recalling and recording the amazement and delight of the most wonderful honeymoon that was ever granted to mortal man. Uniqua who, to my surprise, I found had never been further from her home than Cosmopoli, was delighted, not childishly, but wonderingly, with everything she saw. The beauty of nature, of art, of architecture, of antiquity filled her with deep happiness, which, oddly enough was merged with her in a deep sensual enjoyment of life. Keenly intelligent and interested in everything she saw, whenever she found herself in surroundings of exceptional beauty, a thrill of passion would come over her which rapidly communicated itself to me, and the wayside scenery of Le Vendée and the Bocage, the ruins of departed civilization, a hundred spots in Western and Southern France where we stopped the car to roam at will, come back to my mind as scenes beautified to memory by the most exquisite physical delights. The natural disturbance of her system in which we made our flight from Cosmopoli, seemed to ripen her physical and mental faculties to the highest point, but whenever this was past, she displayed a power of response to emotional stimuli which I sometimes almost feared would wear her out, but we were determined, "not to climb mountains until we reached them," and lived long days and marvellous nights, unimagined by the most poetic and fantastic dreamers of the East.

It was at Avignon one morning as she was lying in my arms, watching the sun rise through our open window, that she said with her lips on mine:—

"Rex—we are going to have a child."

It needed but that to complete our happiness, though from that moment the joy we had in one another became more reasonable, perhaps a little less passionate. I could always rouse her to an ecstasy of desire by caressing and playing with the wonderful masses of hair under her arms, and, her desire appeased, could always soothe her to sleep by the same means. But her passion for me, as a male, had to some extent given place in her to a fierce maternity. As soon as she knew that she was pregnant—she never had any doubt about it—she wrote announcing her news to her mother, and we anxiously awaited her reply, for we felt that this would put the finishing touch to her mother's forgiveness, and reconcile her to the marriage she had so strenuously opposed. A week passed by, and then I received a telegram from my co-trustee. It said:—

"Mrs. Clayton has died suddenly under distressing circumstances. Please return at once."

I was horrified, and wondered how I should break the news to Uniqua. We were sitting in the Palace of the Caesars, quite alone that afternoon, and I thought it a good opportunity. I began:—

"Darling—I have had bad news to-day."

"Have we got to go back?—I shan't mind much, I've got my baby"—she always talked of it as if it were already born.

"No darling," I replied, "it's about your mother."

She looked at me quite gravely, and said:

"Is she dead?"

I could not help feeling a little shocked. She might have been asking if lunch was ready. I began:—

"You must not take it too much to heart. You have got me—"

"And I've got my baby, what does anything else matter? When do we go home?"

I was chilled, but in the circumstances it was better that she should take it like this, than that she should suffer paroxysms of grief. She accepted the situation quite calmly. When I told her she should now have £600 a year of her own, she said:—

"I shall not have to spend any of it, shall I? You are quite rich. I shall save it all for my baby." She never said "our baby".

Then she said: "Do you think Professor Barrowdale was my father?"

This was a blow between the eyes, and I said rather lamely:—

"Well, I have often wondered about it myself, but he never told me anything about it. Did your mother never say anything about your father?" I was curious that we had never touched upon this subject before.

"No," she answered. "I never asked her but once, and then she seemed dreadfully upset, and said I must never speak to her about my father. She could not bear to think about it." After a pause she added, "I don't think Professor Barrowdale was my father—I never felt like it, and I don't think I should have, if—. He seemed more interested in me, and how I got on with lessons and things, and how I was growing up, than really fond of me. Sometimes I fancied that he disliked me—that I 'repugged' him," (one of her words), "but anyhow he must have been an awfully good man. See how he looked after us."

"He *was* a good man," I answered stoutly, "no one ever knew what a lot of fine things he did. Especially for women—the sort of women you have never heard of, women who had come to grief, and were down and out."

"Do you mean prostitutes?"

I was ceasing to be amazed at my wife's sudden remarks, which from time to time showed an esoteric knowledge of the world, gathered I am at a loss to know how or whence.

"Well," I said, "that is about it."

"I don't wonder he was so good to them. It seems awful for men to be so down upon girls who are what I should have been—and proud of it—if you hadn't married me. After all, they are responsible, aren't they?"

"Perhaps."

"And yet I don't know. I wanted you so frightfully the moment I saw you, that you could not have helped having me. No one can say you seduced *me*!"

And thereupon this amazing girl turned to other subjects as if this had been an ordinary dinner-party conversation. But I never loved her more than I did then, or, for that matter, more than I do now. In truth I could reply when, as she often did, she asked me, "How much do you love me, Rex?"

"A little more than I did yesterday, but not so much as I shall to-morrow."

And then by a three days' journey, for I was anxious in the circumstances that she should travel easily, we came back to London, and the world crashed into ruins around me, and the light went out of my life for ever. *Ich habe geliebt und gelebt.*

※

We arrived one evening of the late summer, and put up at the same hotel as that which sheltered us when we fled from Cosmopoli, and next morning I called upon my co-trustee, who received me with grave and forbidding formality. It was clear from his manner that he regarded me as a perverter of youth, and incidentally as a murderer. I tried to open the conversation upon conventional lines.

"This is a most unfortunate circumstance," I began.

He interrupted me. "It is more than unfortunate, it is deeply tragic."

"You mean?"

"Professor Magley," he replied, "it is not my duty, nor have I the inclination, to sit in judgement upon your actions, or even to express an opinion, though, of course, I hold an opinion which I should be loath to express. I will confine myself to the facts. When you—eloped is, I believe, the technical expression—with Mrs. Clayton's daughter, she came up to town and saw me. She was quite dazed—stunned—by what she termed the catastrophe. I will admit that she seemed to regard your action with a horror which, bad as it was, appeared to me exaggerated, seeing that you had repaired your fault, as far as it could be repaired, by rapid marriage. She bitterly blames herself for having so far relaxed her vigilance as to make the meeting between yourself and our ward possible, but the extraordinary, if I may say so, the indecent rapidity with which these events took place made it impossible for her to 'do her duty' as she expressed it. What may have been that duty, and what the views entertained by herself, and by the late Professor Barrowdale as to her daughter's future may be, I cannot conjecture, nor did she enlighten me, but I gathered that she had solemnly sworn to prevent her daughter's marriage if it were possible, by the revelation of certain facts known only to herself and the late Professor. Of what these may have been I have no idea, but I gather that they are contained in a written statement which it becomes my duty to deliver to you. I saw her no more after this interview, but I went down to Cosmopoli to see after her affairs and to attend the inquest."

"The inquest!"

"Yes—you have not seen the papers this morning?"

"No—I arrived last night, and came straight here this morning."

"It took place yesterday, and her remains were buried in the Parish Churchyard yesterday afternoon. It was her wish that neither you nor her daughter should see her again—she was right—it was no sight for a young woman who expects to become a mother."

"Then you know?"

"Yes. One moment. I learned from her servant that on receipt of a letter from our ward in which she announced her condition Mrs. Clayton spent two days without moving from her chair, refusing to eat, or to see such neighbours as she had admitted to a slight acquaintance. On the morning of the third day the servant entering the sitting-room which this unhappy lady had not left, found her lying upon the divan which was soaked in her blood. She had cut her throat—inexpertly—with a common penknife; she must have bled slowly to death, the windpipe was not severed, and the jugular vein only just sufficiently wounded to allow the blood to escape—comparatively slowly. She had left a letter for me which you had better read."

He handed me a sheet of paper scrawled over with incoherent sentences. It said:—

> I cannot face it, I am a coward—I knew I should be when the time came. I ought to have—but I had no chance. I am going to kill myself. I cannot face Uniqua, she must never know. I promised Paul B. that when a man wanted to marry her I would give him the papers. I had no time—if I had had time I know I could not. Mr. Magley must see them, no one else, not even you. You have them, the packet I gave you when Paul B. died. He will understand. What he will do—I forgive him, it wasn't his fault, it was my fault, he will understand when he reads. God help him—and her. *It must not be.*
>
> Ursula Clayton.

"What does it mean?" I asked in a voice which I hardly recognized as my own.

"I do not know. But, Professor Magley, I own that I am terrified, and that I am deeply sorry for you. Paul Barrowdale was a strange man. There were episodes in his earlier life that no one knew about—and what I could guess from collateral evidence and an occasional hint which he dropped, appalled me, hardened as I am by a long professional career to the wilder aberrations of the

31

human mind. Not that Paul Barrowdale was mentally affected—no one was ever more sane, but—he indulged what seemed to me to be terrible and morbid curiosities. Though my views as to your conduct remain unaltered, believe me, I am deeply sorry for you, for I fear that the punishment of your crime—I put it as high as that—may be almost more than any human being should be called upon to bear. Mind! I know nothing, I can only guess, and my brain reels when I allow myself to wander into conjecture. I will now give you the packet of papers to which Mrs. Clayton refers in her letter. I had some difficulty in keeping them from the Coroner on the grounds of professional confidence, and that the papers were not hers but Barrowdale's, and consequently the property of yourself and me as his Executors."

And with that the lawyer handed me a large square envelope sealed at every flap with Paul Barrowdale's private seal.

"If I may add a word of advice," continued he, "I would earnestly beg you not to open this envelope until you and your wife are settled in whatever house you have provided, or will provide, for her. Until that is done you will require all your presence and concentration of mind. I will not hide from you the fact that these incidents are likely to have a significant influence upon your career and position in the University."

My mouth was dry as a morphinomaniac's—I felt deathly cold to the tips of my fingers and toes. I felt that my world was collapsing and that I was being buried in the wreck and ruin of forces of which I was utterly ignorant.

I hardly know how I got back to Uniqua. Fortunately she was quite calm, and showed no curiosity as to my co-trustee. A few days passed during which I went down to Cosmopoli and took a small furnished house in the town, and instinctively I engaged the girl who had been in Mrs. Clayton's service to come and attend to us. Whether it was an effect of the nervous tension in which I was living, the sense of impending horror—conscience if you will—I do not know, but it seemed to me as if the few acquaintances whom I met looked curiously, and askant upon me, avoided me rather. My one object now was to get settled, and to know the worst.

I brought Uniqua down to Cosmopoli, where she took to her new abode like a cat to a new and comfortable basket. She never mentioned her mother—my precautionary warning to the servant not to go into details with the ineradicable gusto of her class was unnecessary. Uniqua did not go out at all, she lay most of the day on the divan which I had installed in conformity with what I knew to be her inclination, and did not appear to notice that in these days passion was utterly dead within me. At night she curled up by my side with her arms and legs wound round me as if I had been a sister to her, and slept peacefully whilst I lay awake listening to the University clocks and praying for daylight.

I put off the opening of Paul Barrowdale's envelope from day to day—*I was afraid!* I told myself that I must get my nerves into stable condition before I undertook the perusal of—what?

❋

The time came however when I pulled myself together and determined to solve the mystery, and one evening—it was about a month ago—when Uniqua had gone to bed I broke the seals. I read. And all the time—continuously it seemed to me, the University clocks cut off and flung into 'the rag-bag of the past, section after section of my life.

### *The Manuscript of Paul Barrowdale.*

This must be written. Some day a man may want to marry Uniqua, *and he must know*. I am sorry for him, whoever he may be, but he must know. With an introduction setting forth the physiological researches which have led to the terrible position of affairs here recorded, I will set down the facts in narrative form.

The study of the physiological phenomena of gestation and reproduction, and the evolution of genera and species has occupied my mind almost exclusively during the whole of my career. Closely connected with this question are the remarkable experiments (and their results) upon the artificial fertilization of parthenogenetic—or to use Lankester's preferable "impaternate"—eggs, carried out by Jacques Loeb, Bataillon, Deslages, and others. The outcome of their researches has seemed to prove incontestably that the function of the male spermatozoön in the fertilization of the female ovum is, in the first place, purely mechanical. They have fertilized and brought up to a pronounced stage of development the larva, and even to relative maturity, parthenogenetic (impaternate) eggs of Echinoderms and Batrachians, by means of artificial stimuli, such as hypertonic solutions, pricking with a fine needle, brushing with camel-hair brushes, to cite in a generalized form only a few of the methods employed in the laboratories of Science. Those who would know more of this are referred to the many papers published on the subject in scientific journals, and of late in the text-books. We start therefore from the conclusion that the action of the spermatozoön is primarily mechanical; it merely perforates and excites the ovum, and "sets it going," so to speak, and may therefore be replaced by artificial and mechanical means.

This being so, we may turn to the theory which deeply occupied the mind of Alphonse Milne-Edwards during the later years of his life. The question arises, why should there be any limits to the possibility of miscegenation? We know that, within a genus, allied species can breed together, as for example a horse with a donkey, a tiger with a jaguar, a fox with a dog—instances might be largely multiplied. But genera cannot breed with genera, as for example a dog with a cat, a horse with a hyena, or an elephant with a rhinoceros—to carry it to the highest point, a man with a mare, a woman with a dog. Why not? If the action of the male spermatozoön is mainly mechanical, why not? This was the problem which occupied the mind of Milne-Edwards and he discussed it with Ray Lankester shortly before his death, and Lankester has recorded his impressions of the discussion in one of his later volumes of collected scientific essays. I will transcribe here his account of the matter. He says:—

"He (Milne-Edwards) held it to be probable, as many physiologists would agree, that the fertilization of the egg of one species by the sperm of another, even a remotely related one, is ultimately prevented by a chemical incompatibility—chemical in the sense that the highly complex molecular constitution of such bodies as the anti-toxins and serums with which physiologists are beginning to deal is 'chemical'—and that all the other and secondary obstacles to fertilization can be overcome or evaded in the course of experiment. He proposed to inject one species with 'serums' extracted from the other, in such a way as seemed most likely to bring the chemical state of their reproductive elements into harmony, that is to say, into a condition in which they should not be actively antagonistic but admit of fusion and union. He proposed, by the exchange of living and highly organised fluids (by means of injection or transfusion) between and male and a female of separate species, to assimilate the chemical constitution of one to that of the other, and thus probably so to affect their reproductive elements that the one tolerate and fertilize the other."

In this case, observe that the influence of the male spermatozoön would be more than merely mechanical, the male would transmit his physical characteristics to the zygote—the embryothus called into existence. When the Sea-urchin's (*Echinus*) eggs to which I have referred above, are pierced (as is done in laboratory experiments), by the sperm filaments of Feather-star (*Comatula*) introduced for the purpose in another series of experiments, the sperm filaments pierce the egg-coat but contribute no substance to the embryo into which the egg develops.

They merely "stimulate" it and set changes going. But if physiological technique could be perfected to such a point as to harmonize the fluids of the Feather-star with those of the Sea-urchin we should, or might, get a hybrid between Comatula and Echinus.

To adumbrate is at once an ultimate result to be aimed at. How often we find a splendid young woman married to a physically perfect young man, keenly anxious to have babies and carrying out to the full their privileges towards that end—but they remain childless. It is clear that their serums are toxic to one another. The man has a passing affair with a servant-girl or shop-assistant, and she immediately has a baby; the woman gives herself sporadically to a lover and immediately conceives: they have found their natural "affinity." There is in my opinion a great future in store for the bold surgeon or physiologist who will rectify matters in these "sterile" marriages, by bringing the husband and wife into a condition of mutual equilibrium by injection, inoculation or transfusion as suggested by Milne-Edwards.

How is this to be done, and how are the facts to be established? The answer comes to us from the Physiologist's Laboratory, and from the clinic. How often one reads in the newspapers, and even in novels, of devoted friends who have offered themselves, when a comrade is suffering from severe hæmorrhage (and in other circumstances), for transfusion of blood. Sometimes we are told that in spite of the heroism of the friend, the patient has died— in nine cases out of ten it is, or was, because of that heroic gift of the friend; the patient has been killed, as surely as if the operating surgeon had blown out his brains.

The War-hospitals of 1914-18 afforded us, first examples, then experiments, and at last lessons, which, once learned, have abolished the grave danger attending transfusion of blood from one human being to another. It has been established that in this matter the human subject is divided into four classes, between which phenomena are varied. If a drop of blood from the donor and recipient are mixed upon a microscope slide, the corpuscles either swim about freely together in the mixed serum—in which case the operation may be safely performed—or, haemolysis (agglutination) takes place. The corpuscles "clot" together, and we know that, if the operation is proceeded with, the recipient will be almost immediately killed. Before the dawn of this knowledge, how many patients may have fallen victims to the "heroism" of a toxic friend? To make this matter clearer, if you are not already familiar with it, I will reproduce here the diagram from Back and Edward's *Textbook of Surgery* (p.79):—

Serum

|  |  | 1 | 2 | 3 | 4 |
|---|---|---|---|---|---|
| | 1 | o | + | + | + |
| Corpuscules | 2 | o | o | + | + |
| | 3 | o | + | o | + |
| | 4 | o | o | o | o |

In the case marked "+" agglutination takes place. In the cases marked "o" no agglutination takes place. Thus it will be seen that the blood of group 4 may safely be given to *any* recipient—they are the "universal donors." The serum of group 1 does not agglutinate when mixed with that of any of the others—they are the "universal recipients." But give the blood (say) of group 3 to a patient of group 2 and you will kill the patient.

In the case of the sterile marriages a simple blood test of this kind will establish the facts upon which the surgeon may safely proceed.

You will wonder—whoever you are, who is destined to read this manuscript—why I have delayed my narrative by this long scientific introduction. It is in the nature of an "*apologia*," in the classical sense of the word, for what follows.

As a young man, and beyond that time, I made many experiments to prove the truth of this theory—many of which were entirely successful. I produced hybrids between widely separated genera, which often shocked even myself. I did not dare to publish my researches to the world, the time was not ripe—the scientific outlook was not yet sufficiently broad. Negligent as I was, almost to the point of fearlessness, of public opinion, I shrank from the howls of ignorant rage which would have greeted the publication of my results. The anti-vivisection mania was at its height. Foul libels upon the earnest workers at physiological research found ready publication in the Press, and it was tacitly understood among physiologists that our experiments must for the most part be kept to ourselves. University authorities looked ever with an anxious eye upon the biological laboratories, ever anticipating the eruption of some sensational scandal or subversive theory, which would rouse a storm of ill-informed invective against the scientific teaching of the Universities. But in my private laboratory—which became a veritable zoological garden—I never relaxed my efforts.

You will not be surprised—even though you be shocked—at what I am going to say next. I looked forward, as the crowning experiment of my career, to the production of a hybrid between one of the higher forms of the Animal world—and Man. You must realise my position. The sexual union of human beings and animals is, no doubt properly, shuddered at, as perhaps the foulest form of unnatural crime. It figures in our books of jurisprudence under the name of "Bestiality," a felony punishable until comparatively recent years with death, and actually with penal servitude for life. How could a man in my position put himself into the power of a man who would lend himself to so "filthy" an experiment? The widely varying forms of Sodomy were looked upon as "aberrations," but were none the less punished by long terms of imprisonment, but Bestiality was regarded as an even lower and more revolting form of vice. The accomplice would necessarily be of the lowest order of criminal, and one would have laid himself open to everlasting blackmail. The suggestion is obvious that I might have been an active participator in the "experiment." I will only say that my whole soul revolted from the idea with shuddering disgust, and I should—to put it on no higher grounds—have been physically impotent in approaching the subject from a personal point of view. I read the horrible treatise on the subject of Dubois-Dessaules published in 1705, and my gorge rose at the long catalogue of horrors he had resuscitated from the Morgue of forgotten criminal records.

Bestiality, as a crime, dates from the highest antiquity. In the more outspoken early editions of our Bible it is indicated, *haud incerta voce*, as rife among the Jews both male and female, and the references to it in Exodus and Leviticus are explicit.[1] In Mythology it appears as a common ruse among Gods, who appear to have found it easier to seduce the daughters of men metamorphosed as animals, than clothed in their normal and god-like attributes; the legends of Phoebus and the Lesbian Issa, of Pasiphaë, of Leda, of Io, are prominent examples among the Metamorphoses of Ovid. In the Middle Ages the Devil is constantly taking the form of a goat for the purposes of sexual connexion with reputed Witches. The work of Boguet upon the Sorcerers (1607) teems with examples, and gives categoric instances of women who have been fecundated by dogs, whilst the laborious compilation of Dubois-Dessaules runs to 450 pages of revolting record. The works of Voltaire bristle with instances on record of the resultant birth of the monsters. In India, sculptures on the Temples of Shiva, especially at Orissa, represent continually the sexual conjugation of women with apes, dogs and other animals. The Criminal Codes of Prussia, Germany and the United States recognise the crime, that of Pope John XIII provided for its "accommodation" but a fine of 250 livres. The historians Aelian and Athenaeus cite numerous instances as a mere matter of record, and as lately as 1882 Lacassagne has produced a work *La*

---

1 Exodus, XXII. 19. Leviticus XVIII. 24 and XX. 15, 16.

*Criminalité chez les Animaux.* As active or passive agents, human beings form a long procession down the records of Jurisprudence, and the work upon the subject of Tardieu is well-known to Pathologists, Alienists and Jurists. As a rule the crime was included under the general heading of "Sodomy," but the earlier jurists drew a sharp distinction, e.g. A. de Liguori who gives the definition *"Sodomia, i.e. cum persona ejusdem sexus; et Bestialitas, i.e. concubitus cum bestia."*

Bestiality as a deliberate inclination is classed by Krafft-Ebing with Sadism, Flagellation, Exhibitionism, Necrophily, and Homosexuality under the general heading of Paresthesia, and the scientific attitude towards these aberrations may be summed up as follows:—Too many different factors concur to produce races for it to be possible to unify, to codify, human morality. Heredity, climate, education, social conditions, riches or poverty, each of these contributes a different factor. The Human Creature is not always master of his functions, his existence depends upon inimical or allied factors against which it is sometimes impossible for him to re-act. Therefore, in the face of the worst turpitudes of human nature, known to us as crime or vice, the Scientist does not protest, he merely seeks for the causes and tabulates the effects.

Undoubtedly the dominating factor is heredity, and Tardieu goes even further than this in ascribing such aberrations to atavism, and we find the records of such factors in every corpus of legend and tradition from the Golden Ass of Apuleius down to the bestialities of the Arabian Nights; from the references of Nicolas de Venette to those of Montaigne, and of Balzac, of Armand Charpentier and others. Among savage races we have the amazing records of Paul du Chaillu dating from comparatively modern times. With loathsome "romances" of de Musset (Gamiani), Bishops and of other Pornographers we have not to concern ourselves. This rapid historic review has seemed to be necessary as an indication of the lines along which this horrible subject may be pursued and studied, should it be required to do so.

There have been many cases recorded of Bestiality in which women have been the passive human participants—they in fact constitute the majority of recorded instances, obviously by reason of the fact that, in such cases, the reasoning human participant is not called upon for action. These are no less horrifying than the others, but it was clear that to find such a woman one would have to ply a muck-rake among the ranks of the lowest, most abandoned, and depraved members of the prostitute class—one had heard of such things in the brothels of Paris, Berlin and Naples. I shrank from the bare idea of encountering such creatures. I had experimented successfully in artificial fecundation with the lower animals—but when I considered the possibility of carrying this higher, I found myself confronted with the same insuperable feeling of horror and repulsion. But none the less, theoretically, the thing became an *idée fixe* in my mind—an *ultima ratio* probably never destined to get beyond the theoretical stage.

This brings me down to a moment—now fourteen years ago—which, in the success of achievement, has cast a shadow over the whole of my remaining life.

I had read so far in Barrowdale's manuscript, and at this point I sprang to my feet, overcome with a hideous nausea; I felt that I was fainting from sheer terror and apprehension. What was I going to read? I put down the MS., took a stiff dose of brandy and walked out into the night air, to think, to recover my senses, to overcome the horror that was gripping me. I had almost determined to read no further, when a fearful thought crossed my mind. It will probably have crossed the reader's. I tried to put it from me in vain—it simply tortured me physically—*but I knew I must read on.* After an hour I returned home. I crept up to our bedroom. Uniqua was sleeping peacefully, her delicious smile just parting her perfect lips. I reassured myself for a moment, and then fell back again into my previous mood of terror and consternation. Whatever I was to read, I had brought it upon myself, and I went back to the damned MS.

### (The MS. Continued.)

I used to get the animals which served me for my research work down at the Docks—from the successors of the renowned Jamrach. They thought, and I did not undeceive them, that I was an agent of the Zoological Society. One day I visited my purveyor in answer to a note informing me that he had a remarkable splendid specimen of

*Felis jubata*, the Indian Hunting Leopard or Cheetah, an animal I had long desired to possess, on account of its curious capacity for being domesticated and kept as a pet. It was a most beautiful beast, a male about a year old which had been bred in captivity, and was already as docile and as responsive to caress as any ordinary cat. I bought him and made arrangements for his transfer to my house in the country where I kept my creatures. The few colleagues who were admitted to a knowledge of my experiments called it my "Island of Dr. Moreau"—from the late H.G. Wells's dreadful book of that title. Not, however, that my work had anything even remotely in common with the horrors suggested in that remarkable work. By the use of general and local anaesthetics my animals were never alarmed, or indeed conscious that they were what the Anti-Vivisectionists would have called "Martyrs to Science"—they were a very happy family, and, in point of fact, when they had spent their allotted time with me and had bred the desired hybrid, or failed to do so, in ease and comfort, I transferred them to Regent's Park. No animal ever died under my care or treatment, except from pneumonia or some other disease incidental to our climate, or to the artificial conditions of its existence.

I was returning late in the afternoon up Ratcliffe Highway, speculating upon the motley crowd of seafaring folk of all nations that throng that historic thoroughfare, and the degraded types of harlot who ply their wretched trade among them, when one of these, giving my arm a gentle nip as she passed me, said, in a half-whisper:—

"D'you want a naughty girl?"

I looked at her as I shrugged her off. She was a finely made, bold-looking strumpet, younger in years and it seemed to me of a higher racial type than the generality of the local consorority. Very fair, neatly though shabbily dressed, with large wistful grey eyes, and teeth that were both clean and regular. Her appearance surprised me. My short scrutiny encouraged her and she said rapidly:

"I'm the naughtiest girl in the Highway, and I like old gentlemen. I'll do anything, show you anything you like. Don't you want to come with me? I'll astonish you."

"Go to the devil," I said brutally, "or I'll give you in charge."

"All right, Governor," she replied. "I'm going. *Au revoir, mon ami,*" and before I could recover from my surprise at her accent, which was perfect, she flung herself on the rails in front of a rapidly approaching tram-car.

Deeply shocked, and responding to an irresistible instinct, I flung myself after her, caught her by one ankle, and jerked her free of the lines. The driver had applied his brakes, but the front wheels crushed her hat. It was the nearest thing possible. I hauled her on to the pavement and immediately a dense crowd of loafers, seafarers and street-walkers collected round us. She had fainted.

"Give us a little room," I said, "I am a doctor. Does anybody know anything about her?"

"Know anything?" ejaculated a sailor, "yes we all know all there is to know, and that's too much—the dirty bitch."

"Oh lor!" chimed in a loathsome and pustular female who had forced her way to the centre of the crowd, "the gent's in luck, ain't he? He's got Menagerie Sal!"

"Whatever she is," I replied hotly, "she can't be left here. Where does she live?"

"Anywhere you like to take her," said another Brute. "Here, get up Sal!" and he kicked her in the side.

I sprang up and would have collared the beast but, perhaps fortunately, the invariable and imperturbable policeman appeared among us, and the crowd fell back.

"Who—what is she?" I asked the man in blue.

"One of the worst, sir, about the worst I reckon." The woman was coming round. "Here, get up Sal," continued the constable, "and go home, if you've got one—or I'll take you."

"I am a doctor," I said quickly, and gave him my card. "Whatever she is, I can't leave her alone in this state— Help me to take her in here."

There was an eating-house just where this occurrence had taken place, and, aided by the constable, I got the woman inside and sat her down in a corner box. The crowd dispersed. As they did so, a draggled harlot called out:—

"The old gent's in for it all right—good luck to him!" And the strange sobriquet was bandied from foul mouth to foul mouth—"Menagerie Sal—Menagerie Sal!"

I sent for some brandy and sat, looking at her as she gradually recovered her self-possession, without saying a word. At last she gave utterance to a short hoarse laugh, and said:—

"What the hell did you do it for? You told me to go there, and I tried to. Yer don't *want* me; what did yer stop me for?"

"True," I said, "I don't want you, but I couldn't let you kill yourself before my eyes. I'm a man, not a brute."

"All men are brutes," she said defiantly.

There was a most extraordinary struggle of accents in her speech. She spoke the low cockney vernacular with fluency and emphasis, but occasional words, intonations, seemed to jar against the vulgarity of the rest of it.

"Not all," I replied. "Myself for instance. Now look here. I'll turn your own question on you—what did *you* do it for?"

"What's that to you?"

"It is a good deal. You are too young and healthy to want to die, however beastly your life may be. Whilst there's life there's hope. You are worth saving."

"Saving! My Gawd! let me up and out of this. You're a bloody gospeller, that's what you are. You're going to talk about the Temple of my Body, and Gawd and that. I ain't a Temple, it's a Cesspool, and there ain't no Gawd. Let me go!"

"I am not a gospeller, and I don't want to preach to you; but I'm a doctor and I want to know what it all means."

"It means that I'm down and out—I've stuck it long enough. You heard what they call me 'Menagerie Sal' (she pronounced 'Menagerie' perfectly) I'm too low down for any self-respecting whore to speak to—I can't get a lodging except in a Chinks' Dive, and I can't get a man unless he's a stranger in these parts—that's why I clawed you— or a right down utter beast of a heathen."

"You are in a wildly hysterical state—that's evident. Now look here, I've saved your life and you belong to me until I've done with you." The wretched creature turned on a "professional" smile. "Don't misunderstand me—I'm not going to have you, but I'm going to make you eat something—hungry?"

"I don't know—I ought to be. I know I've been empty as a drum for two days. I wonder what you're getting at?"

"Nothing in particular," I replied, "but you are going to have some food. We can't sit here and do nothing for the good of the house."

I ordered some food, which arrived, coarse, but plain and good, and she ate sparingly—and with a strange refinement contrasting remarkably with her vocabulary. When she would eat no more, I lit a pipe and gave her a cigarette. She had calmed down.

"Now look here," I said again; "do you feel anything like gratitude to me for what I've done!"

"No, I don't," she replied; "but that doesn't matter. There are other ways. I'll do it when there's no interfering Toff around."

"No you won't. You are going to promise me not to do it again."

She looked me straight in the face without speaking, her chin resting on her hand, puffing cigarette smoke quietly, so as not to reach me. At last I said, "Well?" She replied, "Shut up! I'm thinking."

"A penny for your thoughts!"

"I'll take the penny. I want one. You couldn't make it a shilling, I suppose?"

I laid a sovereign on the table. "Will that help you out a bit?" I asked.

"Haven't seen one for years. Ta, Governor." And she deftly slipped the coin into her stocking and resumed her scrutiny of my face.

"You haven't told me your thoughts—and I've paid," I suggested.

And then I experienced the shock which Balaam must have felt when his Ass addressed him. She took her cigarette from her lips and said quite slowly and without a trace of cockney accent:—

"You look like an intelligent man—I should say a scientist of sorts—not many doctors are scientists down this way. How can you be such an idiot as to ask me to promise you not to do it again? Do you remember what that girl, Wade, in 'Little Dorrit' said to the champion ass Clennam? (by the way I've often wondered if Dickens knew he was describing a Lesbian)—you know—about people who are all the time coming to meet us from strange places along strange roads, and what they'll do to us, and we to them will all be done? Whether I do it again or not has nothing to do with me, it depends at the moment upon you, or rather upon the puny little part you happen to be playing in the inexorable progress of inevitable consequences."

I was dumbfounded! It was my turn to sit and gaze at her. "This way and that, dividing the swift mind"—and she, taking up my case from the table where I had laid it, took a new cigarette, lit it, said "Thank you", and resumed her position, her chin on her hands, looking at me.

At last I said: "How in God's name have you come to this?—you are too good—"

"Oh! Don't begin that—that's what that the Missioners to Fallen Women begin with. And don't bring in God—unless you feel the need of him for conversational emphasis—or convenience, like Xerxes at the end of a rhyming alphabet."

"Let's put it on the lowest grounds then. You are a woman of some education evidently—and, permit me to say—of some refinement. You are too good for Ratcliffe Highway. If prostitution is your vocation in life, why not practise in the West End? Why not the Empire or the Alhambra?" (The "promenades" at these places had not been closed in those days).

"Never mind when or where I started—that's none of your business. I came to grief on a P. and O. steamer—I'd had lots of men—some of the best; but coming home once from China I fell madly in love with a Lascar. A common ship's hand—a bronze god. I wanted him—and I seduced him, it didn't take much doing—I had some money then—but I was ashamed (I was capable of it then) to take him up West. I joined him down here. I used to go up West myself sometimes—no one here knew it—when I was just longing for love—real love—a woman."

"A woman?"

"Yes—for a real lover, or mistress. Oh! don't look shocked; if you're a doctor you know women can love a woman better than any man on earth."

"Then—among other things—you are a—"

"Lesbian—don't be afraid to say it."

"But I don't understand how you—"

"It's easy enough. Men don't hear of the brothels where women can have anything they want and can pay for, from a vicious flapper of fifteen to an insatiable Messalina of fifty. The only difference between those, and—the others—is that all the 'staff' are amateurs; some shop-girls and clerks, but mostly gentlewomen. You've never heard of No. 100, Canterbury Square have you?—no, it's kept pretty quiet—but I didn't go there, I preferred to find my own romances."

"Romances!"

"Yes—can't you imagine the delight, after the brutes down here, of meeting eyes in an omnibus, of a thigh pressed against yours, of a foot that touches yours as if by accident? Of seeing a pretty shop-girl go scarlet when you squeeze her hand as she hands you a parcel? A few ordinary words—a suggestion of meeting again, and then tea together somewhere, and, later, dinner and a night spent in love that leaves you shattered and sleepy and dreaming for days?"

"It seems horrible to me."

"That's because you are a man and don't know what love—really exquisite love—means. Very few men do—but when they do they're divine!"

"But did you not horrify them—at first?"

"Never. We know one another in a flash. The most wonderful love I ever had was a girl of nineteen—the daughter of a peer—Oh! She had been to a good school—a finishing school—it finished her, I can tell you. I got to know her people. Oh! yes, I can be a gentlewoman when I like, and I took her away into the country for a week. I bet you she remembers it, as I do. And then—back to my brute. He'd have been after me otherwise (he thought I'd gone to get more money), and then there would have been hell—and blackmail. So long as my money lasted we lived in a fairly decent set of rooms, and we had a wonderful time, but my God! he was a brute; he thrashed me sometimes—I loved it. And vicious!—I don't want to make your hair stand on end. I'd read a lot of filthy books here and abroad and I thought I knew what vice was. The things he did to me—and that he made me do! I tell you the Five Cities of the Plain rolled into one were a Trappist Monastery compared to our flat. And his friends that he brought to me—and their animals—you people west of Chancery Lane can't dream what are the vices among the Lascars, Chinamen, Malays, half-breed Spanish-Americans, Niggers, Mulattos of all kinds. One didn't know at the end of an orgy whether one was a girl, or a boy, or a beast. Lucky animals can't breed with humans."

A strange, bitter smile flickered over her lips.

"Now my friend," she continued recklessly, "you know what you've 'saved'. You heard what they called me—Ménagerie Sal."

Literally my hair did stand on end. At least, I felt a cold contraction of the scalp, and my sight vacillated.

"This is too horrible. How could you—why did you—stand it?"

"I liked it."

"What?"

"I don't want you to take home any illusions about a repentant sinner. And I've paid for it—my God! I have paid for it. When my money was gone—I had quite a good deal and it lasted a longish time, I sank, if one could sink below that—but one is always comparatively up, when one can pay; I sank lower and lower, the most vicious of the Scum knew of me all over the world, and came to me like filings to a magnet. It was too late to get away. I was 'Ménagerie Sal'—the Darling of the Beasts—human and otherwise—and that's where I am now. I told you the truth just now when I said that no self-respecting whore would be seen speaking to me—and if any clean white man showed any signs of wanting me, they are all round me and on to him—at once—telling him things—mostly true—and what's more, none of them would go with a man if they knew he'd been with me. You know there are grades of respectability even among harlots—I am afraid I am shockingly *mal vue* in the oldest profession in the world, even as practiced in Ratcliffe Highway! It is not often that I have enough to eat—I shouldn't be allowed in here if you hadn't brought me. Now you know why I am going to kill myself. If I don't, one of the brutes will kill me some day. See this scar?" and she pulled her blouse away upon her shoulder, "that was done by a sort of Gorilla—I was trying to get away from him. So I am going to 'out it'—don't you think I'm right?"

I could not answer. I was paralysed with horror, especially by the calm manner with which she spoke of these unspeakable atrocities. I harked back, and repeated in an undertone:—

"You like it!"

"Yes—sometimes—that's the truth. But I'm afraid of the end of it—afraid!" and she covered her face with her hands and shuddered.

I sat looking at her—at last, as though she were a curious pathological case in a mental Hospital. And then a horrible but irresistible thought came into my mind. The Cheetah!

※

I began, my heart beating violently, to feel my way.

"What a life!" I said, "but I confess you interest me dreadfully."

"Do I?" she said suddenly looking up; "Aren't you disgusted?" Then she gave a short laugh and said: "I wonder! Well—I expect you'd be as bad as any of them if you had a chance—if the truth were only known—"

"And suppose I were?"

"Oh! I shouldn't mind—I've been through too much. But I *am* surprised—you with your solemn learned old air."

I thought rapidly, and then, to my eternal misery, I made up my mind. Such a chance could never occur again. I said:—

"Supposing I *were* a worn out old rake, with unnameable curiosities? Jaded with all ordinary vices? And supposing I said to you, 'Come away from here, come and live in the country. I'll settle a sum of money upon you which will keep you from want in the event of my death. I *am* a Scientist—a vicious one, if you like. I should want to try all kinds of experiments on you.' What would you say?"

"I'd say, as the Yanks do: 'Put it there, Governor.' You can't do anything worse to me than I've had done to me

55

already. And I'd love to be away from all this mob. When do we start?"

We talked on for half-an-hour and then I left her. She gave me an address to write to—at a *Poste Restante*.

A month later she was installed in a cottage in the village where I then had my Research Laboratory. She had no desire to mix with the people of the place, but for the information of the public and the parson, she gave herself out to be a young widow. The name she adopted was Mrs. Clayton. Of course it was immediately observed that she had come there at my instigation, and that when I was at the Laboratory she was constantly at my house. They drew their own—the inevitable—conclusions, but, as I had steadily repelled any attempt on the part of the aborigines to establish social relations with me of any kind, this did not trouble us.

Ursula Clayton left behind her in the parlieus of the Docks every trace of her "professional" career, accent, vocabulary and manner. When my solicitor (who with my assistant Rex Magley will be trustees of my will) had proved to her that a certain income was settled upon her in any event, she abandoned all reserve with me; hitherto our relations had been a trifle strained; she seemed unable to realize that I was determined to act in her permanent interest, and was not merely amusing myself with her for a time. She became a really delightful companion; I was a bachelor, and never at any time an Anchorite, and the society of Ursula Clayton was interesting—and satisfying in every respect. I gradually came to know her history, which, though it does not concern this narrative, is illuminating as an explanation of her abnormal sexuality.

In the eighties of the last century, there are still people old enough to remember, a hot wave of what are known as Unnatural Vices almost openly and unblushingly practiced, swept over our English Society. It was the outcome of the Æsthetic Craze, intimately associated with the name of Oscar Wilde, who ultimately, in the nineties, paid for everyone, and subsequently died overwhelmed with public infamy, and the private admiration of the few. It became a matter of ordinary conversation to discuss homosexual love affairs of men and women prominent in Society—especially of the latter. In a word, Sodomy and Lesbianism were—*sub rosâ*—fashionable. Pre-eminent among the male "perverts" was a well-known Peer of artistic taste and enormous wealth, at whose house in the county homosexualists of both sexes congregated, and where, as was averred, "orgies" took place that were spoken about with bated breath in the most fashionable boudoirs. Prominent in this society was a very high born dame indeed, in whose hands, or arms, no woman was safe, and she formed the centre of a Lesbian *côterie* which spread like a rodent ulcer into almost every class of society. It was in the un-natural order of things that the masculinity of the Lady, and the femininity of the Lord X——, should bring them closely together, so closely indeed that, to the astonishment of the inverted world, Lady Z—gave birth to a child who was christened Ursula. This child was sent abroad, to be brought up in Italy. A respectable sum of money was "settled" for her maintenance and education which became hers absolutely on attaining her majority. With such an heredity it is not surprising that Ursula developed, early, a sexual precocity and *désinvolture*, which the settlement made upon her by her parents enabled her to gratify to the fullest extent of her inclination. She told me her early sexual history, which was amazing, but does not concern us, beyond what she told me in Ratcliffe Highway, and which I have already recorded. By the time she came to "our village" her fires were burning low, her sexuality was to a great extent satiated, and she showed no trace in her manner or proclivities of the storms which had disturbed her youth. She was a charming companion, an intelligent and well-educated friend, and a charming mistress.

And the Cheetah? We called him "Kumar". He settled down in our two houses as a great affectionate domestic pet. Sometimes, in passage between the two, led on a chain by Ursula, he terrified the inhabitants of the village, human and animal, but this was very seldom, and the villagers had grown accustomed to what was known as "the Professor's Zoo." The attachment between "Kumar" and Ursula became very close, and indeed I sometimes feared a precipitation of events, but Ursula was too keenly interested in my work to endanger the results by premature action. I conducted my experiment on the lines suggested by Milne-Edwards; it was nothing to inoculate Kumar under a local anæsthetic—he would never have dreamed of the possibility of being hurt by either of us.

The day arrived when the blood tests were wholly satisfactory. The serum of the one accommodated the corpuscles of the other without any trace of hæmolysis—and I left the rest to Ursula.

※

I do not know what I expected to be the outcome of this experiment. It was impossible to anticipate. As a practising surgeon I was skilled in obstetrics and had no fear for the result, only an intense curiosity. If I expected anything, it was a queer little "monster," which I should allow to live long enough to be perfectly formed, and then "prepare" as a specimen, explaining its presence as an arrival from a native collector in India. At the end of only six months anticipation Ursula gave birth to one of the most perfectly formed little female children it has ever been my lot to look upon. She was remarkably furry, but new-born babies are often thus, and, as in the case of this child, they lose it in a month or two. I should mention, though it is not material, that I took a house on the South Coast for Ursula to await the event. I delivered her myself, and she brought the child, whom we had registered as of illegitimate birth under another name, and had baptized Uniqua—the only apposite name, it seemed to me—back to our village. There could not be any question of destroying so perfect a little specimen of humanity, and when Ursula returned with her, she "explained" her, when necessary as a foundling she had adopted from a workhouse on her travels.

(I will not try to set down here what were my thoughts as I read this frightful record. They are indescribable—it was all I could do to prevent myself burning the MS. and taking five grains of morphine on the spot. But I dared not do it. I had to read on, though it was now broad daylight.)

✹

The child grew in beauty and charm, developing with a rapidity which amazed me. When she was two years old, Ursula Clayton left her cottage and came to live in the house near Cosmopoli where she now inhabits. After the birth of Uniqua I ceased my physiological experiments in this direction—I had been too successful—and dispersed my collection of animals. I was frankly terrified—and still am—at the success of my culminating effort. Uniqua is entirely human physically, but I constantly recognize the feline influence in little actions, tastes—in her whole mentality. *What will happen when she grows up?*—when her sexual life begins, when puberty asserts itself? I tremble to think. One thing is abundantly manifest, she must never be allowed to marry. What response would she make to the Mendelian Law? Her children—*would* they be children? The thought turns me cold. The one thing I can think of is that as soon as she reaches puberty she must be drastically operated upon—ovariotomy, hysterectomy—the whole thing. But how explain the necessity? Would any surgeon in the world consent to "spay"—to sterilise—a perfectly healthy, apparently normal and beautiful young girl? I doubt it very much. There is only one course to be pursued, but it is one which will shatter and ruin my life and Ursula's. So long as we two, and we alone, know the awful secret of Uniqua's birth, our minds may remain easy, and we can face the world with nothing more against us than the tittle-tattle of our neighbours, who may look upon Ursula as the faithful mistress of a faithful bachelor Professor. Indeed I often regret that I did not marry Ursula before I brought her to Cosmopoli—I should then have been able to keep closer watch over Uniqua, and carry out myself what I now set down. If any man ever desires to marry Uniqua, *he must be told the whole truth.* It will be a frightful thing to do and it might have to be done over and over again! It would end by all coming out. But if, in spite of this stunning revelation, any man is bold enough to persist in his desire to marry her, he must be warned to take every possible and known precaution against having children by her.

I may die before this happens, and then—God help her—this awful duty will devolve upon Ursula Clayton. It is with this in view that I have written out this MS. in all its revolting details, concealing nothing, glossing over nothing. Ursula shall do all she can to discourage suitors, but should one present himself persistently, *he must be told.*

I have told him.

PAUL BARROWDALE.
August 19—.

✳

(Following upon this apparent termination of his MS. came another entry dated ten years later.)

✳

I reopen this Record which I ardently hoped I should never peruse again. But it is imperatively necessary. At the age of eleven Uniqua has passed the arrival of puberty and is a fully developed and very beautiful girl, having passed through a stage in which, though beautifully formed, she was a sallow, swarthy, repellent little girl. Her whole body is classically perfect, and as far as showing it to her mother and me is concerned, quite unashamed of her perfect nakedness. She is covered with the light "peach-bloom" down which makes many fair women so intensely attractive, but the down is a light tawny-orange colour, recalling the coat of poor Kumar (who died by my hand, deeply as I regretted the necessity, after her birth). The down is punctuated here and there, at more or less regular intervals, by small imperfect rings of a darker colour (that of her normal hair, though not so dark), which, to our instructed eyes, recall vividly the markings of Kumar's coat. The only idiosyncrasy which she exhibits beyond this is the extraordinary luxuriance of her axillary and pubic hair, which is beautifully grown, but phenomenal in such a young girl. She has another peculiarity which one cannot but recognise as hereditary. If she is unhappy, which is rare, or annoyed, which is rarer still, or if she is afflicted with any passing fit of childish naughtiness, all that is necessary is to insinuate our fingers into the thick curls under her arms and tickle and caress her like an animal. Her mood becomes serene at once, I hate to use the word (knowing what we do), but she positively "purrs" with contentment, and if the caress is gently prolonged she goes fast asleep.

The primary object of this post-scriptum is, however, to call attention to what is really a very serious matter. It is that at her times of periodic disturbance, which take place, not monthly, but at intervals of three to four months, she is subject to what may rightly be called *oestrum*, a frenzy of sexual desire. Though she is technically quite ignorant of sexual matters, it appears in many ways, her beauty is greatly enhanced, her eyes become even finer than usual, her lips more crimson, and her nipples are in a constant state of erection and intense sensitiveness. She is restless and unsatisfied, and wants to go out and mix with people for no reason that she is aware of. As a rule she is self-contained and utterly indifferent to companionship, even to that of her mother. At these times, which are remarkably prolonged—often to a fortnight or three weeks—she must be very carefully watched, above all things she must not be allowed to get into contact with men; I am convinced, poor child, that it would be disastrous to her, and the terrible results I have hinted at in the record would almost certainly ensue. Ursula Clayton is alive to this, and I can rely upon her never to leave her alone in these circumstances. Her husband, should she ever have one, must also be warned of this danger.

I have warned him.

PAUL BARROWDALE.
May, 19—.

It is as impossible for you, who read this, to imagine, as it is for me to describe, what I felt when I at last terminated the perusal of Barrowdale's MS. One amazing fact, one concerning which I had curiously enough evinced no curiosity, was that of her age. Comparing the dates of Barrowdale's Record and its postscript, it became clear, Uniqua was only thirteen years old. It was broad day when I went up to our bedroom. Uniqua had not moved, she lay with her head resting on her right arm, which had drawn her nightdress free of her right breast, which stood up inviting caress. I put my lips to it, and closed them in a long kiss—the delicate intoxicating perfume which I now could explain struck me more persistently than usual. Under my caress she awoke for a moment, and said, "Oh, you darling! then it wasn't a dream. Go on." And so fell asleep in my arms as she rolled over on to me, and slept until the servant brought our morning tea.

After breakfast I told her I had worked until morning and must go for a long walk to get the cobwebs out of my head. She said:—

"All right, so long as you don't ask me to go with you. I shall curl up on the divan and think about my baby."

I went out. Her baby! What would it be? Barrowdale and I had carried out a long series of Mendelian experiments—I could not blind myself to the probability; the inheritance of characteristics transmitted through the female line. That she would "throw back" (I shuddered at the thought) was practically a certainty—a foregone conclusion. There was nothing else for it—abortion is a hideous word, *but this child must not be born*. It must be got rid of at once—she was almost two months pregnant already—I shuddered at the thought of what even a mis-carriage might bring to light. I knew that I had a terrible task before me, but I had to face it. How terrible it was I fortunately could not foresee, or what an effect my decision was to have upon both of us.

I tried to prepare the way by calling upon the doctor whom I had had in my mind as our "Family Physician", a good worthy soul and thoroughly conversant, as a result of long practise, with his job, which was to see people safely into and out of the world, instil common sense into their mothers in dealing with their childish ailments, and to comfort his adult patients by an assumption of knowledge of their "cases" which he was far from pretending, in ordinary conversation, to posses. I had been on terms of friendly social intercourse with him ever since my arrival in Cosmopoli, and I thought that I could count upon him to help me deal with my fearful problem with sympathy and tact. This was the one mistake that I have made throughout my trouble, a mistake which has rendered it necessary for me to be prepared for the worst— for scandal—for exposure, and possibly worse.

I had not realized and appreciated, though I had perceived unmistakable indications of, the feeling that existed in Cosmopoli with regard to my "abduction" of Uniqua and the suicide of Ursula Clayton, which was—in the absence of any possible explanation—the direct result of my action. Dr. Fisher received me with a demeanour which was distant, severe, and almost embarrassed, but though I felt this "in my bones" I persuaded myself that my condition of nervous strain led me to exaggerate the peculiar aloofness of his manner. I hastened to put our interview upon a semi-professional basis.

"I want to have a word with you," I said, "about my wife."

"Yes?" It should have been obvious to me that he was on his guard, and had no intention of meeting me half-way.

"She is very young—much younger indeed than I had any idea of when I married her."

"And yet, you, as Barrowdale's intimate friend, should have known. How old is she?"

I passed this question by, and said:—

"He never spoke to me of his relations with Mrs. Clayton, I only saw the child once before we met accidentally—and fell in love with one another."

He shrugged his shoulders slightly and looked away out of the window. I ought to have seen that he did not believe me.

"I am not satisfied about her health," I went on, blindly, "I have reason to suspect an endometrititis. Until this has been dealt with-surgically—I feel that she ought not to bear children."

He remained quite silent, and I proceeded.

"I do not know whether she would readily submit to examination, but I should like you to make it."

"You have reason to believe she is pregnant." It was a statement rather than a question.

"Yes. And if I am right I think that the pregnancy should be—avoided—for this time at least."

He rose from his chair and Walked to the window, where he remained silent for a minute or so—which seemed to me an eternity—and then turning round but not coming back to his seat, he said:—

"Professor Magley, I will be quite candid with you. You know—or should know if you do not, that there is a very strong feeling prevalent in this town with regard to your action in taking this young girl away from her mother, a feeling which was greatly exacerbated by the terrible sequel which your action brought about. It is not my intention or inclination to sit in judgement upon you, your own conscience is probably dealing with the matter, and I do not envy you your reflections. But now you come to me, and in practically so many words you suggest that I should relieve you of immediate consequences and inconvenience by procuring abortion for you. Please understand me once and for all that I absolutely refuse to have any hand in the matter whatever. If your wife consults me I shall do my utmost to protect her by any means in my power from any attempt of the kind. And before we either of us say anything more—which we might subsequently regret—I think it better that this interview should come to an end. I advise you to forget it, but bear in mind that I shall not."

And he moved to the door which he opened. I can only say that I "slunk" out.

Well—I realized the colossal mistake I had made, and that if anything was to be done, I must depend solely upon myself—and upon Uniqua.

That evening she was lying in my arms on the divan, and, by the familiar resource of caressing her amid her wonderful axillary hair, I had got her into a condition of luxurious and almost passionate happiness. I opened the subject by saying:—

"Are you very keen to have this baby of yours?"

"Indeed, yes, how can you ask it? Imagine what it will be?"

Alas! my imagination was only too active, too precise, and too terrific. I went on:—

"I have been thinking, darling, that we are so intensely happy with one another, that it seems a pity to put a stop to it by having a child at once. Would it not be better for both of us if we waited a little—say a year, during which we can have one another all to ourselves? I am a little jealous of your baby, just at present, though in a year or so—"

"What do you mean?" she said, drawing a little away from me and looking at me, her beautiful eyes wide open, the pupils fully dilated, "We haven't waited—the baby is here."

"Well, hardly," I replied, trying to convey an impression that we were merely discussing a possibility of no great importance. "These things are easily rectified— avoided. Remember, I am a surgeon as well as a doctor of medicine and of science. I could put you right without any difficulty or danger, and practically without discomfort or disturbance to yourself."

She sprang to her feet. "What do you mean?" she repeated.

"Oh, a very simple matter. A drug, perhaps a very slight operation, and we should be as we were before, and could take our own time about having a child. This one—if it can be called a child yet—is, as it were, an unexpected, a premature, accident."

She stood looking at me, with an expression of savage loathing and horror. Her breasts heaved tumultuously, her lips were parted, not in a smile, tumultuously, but in a ghastly rictus, showing her prominent little canine teeth in an evil indescribable grin. Her fingers clawed at the joining of her wrapper which she pulled free from her breasts as if to give herself air, and then she said in a voice I had never heard before, a kind of hissing growl:—

"You—propose—to—me—to—kill—my—baby?"

"Oh! don't put it like that. I only mean—"

"You mean—you mean?—Oh! You brute—you beast—you devil!"

"Darling!" I sprang up and advanced towards her. She flung out her hands, catching me on the chest with such force that I lost my balance, and fell back on the divan. She took a step forward and stood over me.

"Don't touch me—don't come near me—never again—you murderer!"

And she fled from the room. I sprang up and followed her, but I was too late—she had gained our bedroom, slammed the door and locked it, and I heard her rush to the door of my dressing room and lock that also.

"Darling—listen!" I said as loud as I dared—on account of the servants—through the door, "It's all right. I didn't mean it. I promise not to speak of it again. Only come out—or let me in. I *must* speak to you. You have misunderstood me." I was in agony.

After a few minutes, during which I implored her to open the door, I heard her say, still in the raucous voice which had filled me with horror downstairs:—

"If I open the door for a moment and say something, will you promise me upon your honour as a man not to force your way into the room?"

There was no help for it. I promised. Then she opened the door. She had flung off her wrapper and stood, holding the door, clad only in a short *crêpe de chine* chemise, which had slipped down to her waist on one side, being held on the other by a shoulder ribbon. I had never seen her look so superb. And she said, hardly above a whisper:—

"If you force your way in here tonight, I will tear you with my nails. I will bite you—some way or other I will kill you. Perhaps to-morrow I may be able to bear to look at you. Now I must think—leave me alone with my baby."

And she closed the door again and locked it. I went downstairs. The whole horror of the situation burst upon me. *Uniqua had reverted to type.* She was no longer a girl—she was a Cheetah! The animal instinct fiercely awakened in defence of her young was aroused to its highest point. I did not attempt to blind myself to the fact—she had become dangerous. I foresaw a condition of things fraught with all the possibilities of appalling tragedy. To protect her unborn offspring, she was capable of anything—even of killing me. For a moment I wished she would, it would be a happy release for me, but afterwards? Regard being had to her "parentage" it was impossible to tell how long she would carry her young within her; would the period of her gestation be human, or feline? It depended, I felt, upon what was to be born. My scalp contracted with horror at the thought. One thing, and one thing only was clear to me—I must not allow the monster I anticipated to see the light—I must be no party to the perpetuation of a race of hybrid monsters, that might be frightful. And it came to this—I must take precautions that she did not kill me—*I must kill her*. And I loved her as no man has ever loved a woman before—utterly—blindly—and even at that supremely awful moment I desired her beautiful body. I was thirsty to caress—to have her.

I tried to sleep on the divan—worn out as I was—but sleep would not come. I tossed about all night, sometimes going out into the summer night to cool the fever which raged in every limb. I drank. I thought for a moment again of a hypodermic injection of morphia to dull my tortured senses—to forget for a while—but I feared what Uniqua might do if she found me insensible in her present mood. No—I must go through with it and keep my brain clear—my presence of mind at its highest pitch.

Next day Uniqua came down after lunchtime. She recoiled when I would have taken her in my arms.

"Sit down," she said, fortunately in her natural, low, musical voice, "I have something to say to you!"

I sat down and waited. She paced up and down the room—with a curious soft padding step—the Cheetah was dominant. After a while she said:—

"I have thought all night. I know what is in your mind—it's no use to try and reassure me—I have a new instinct—like an animal—a new knowledge—and I can protect myself and my baby. Until it is born—perhaps for always—I will never let you touch me or sleep with me again. I will never be off my guard in your presence. I will take no food which you have had the remotest chance of touching. I will live with you in broad daylight——unless I find it impossible. If I do—I will go away and live upon my annuity where you shall never find me. But you have your work to do here, and I don't want to ruin your career."

Poor child! She little knew how utterly it was ruined already—I hardly knew myself.

It was no use protesting. Her instinct was infallible. For her I was the Enemy, seeking to destroy her and her baby—*and it was true*.

Some weeks have passed since that awful night. As to my own position, I know that my University career is ended, I have only anticipated matters by intimating to the authorities that I retire from the Professorship of Physiology at the end of this term, and already they are looking for my successor.

There are moments when a wave of her old love for me comes over her, and she allows me to caress her lightly—in broad daylight. At the slightest attempt on my part to become demonstratively affectionate she withdraws herself, as cats do when they are bored with the attention of their human companions. I sleep in my dressing room, where I have added interior bolts to the doors. It is a period of armed strain.

But there are times when she allows me to raise one of her arms and play as of yore with her axillary curls, and at these times she is almost off her guard. If my hands wander to her lovely body she comes to herself and flings me off, but it has given me the clue to the ultimate solution. Time is getting on and I must act. I have a hypodermic filled with Aconitine—one day when she is hypnotized by the only caress she allows me, I shall thrust the needle among the roots of the hair under her arm. It will be instantaneous—and undiscoverable. There will be a post-mortem of course. If the opening of the uterus reveals what I fear, professional etiquette will keep knowledge of the discovery from the world. What I shall do then remains to be seen. I now know that Paul Barrowdale was—I cannot call him a coward for I know what he bore through long years—but I know that he inoculated himself with a pure culture of septic pneumonia—and died an apparently natural death.

The scientific importance of the facts which have led to these multiplied tragedies is too great for them to be utterly lost to future Physiologists. I shall deposit this record with Blayre, our Registrar, sealed up with instructions that it is not to be opened until twenty-five years after my death, when a new generation will have forgotten Rex Magley and the scandals which surrounded the closing months of his life.

*Note.*—More than twenty-five—nearly thirty, in fact—years have elapsed since Rex Magley deposited this MS. with me. It was obvious, when he deposited it, that he

73

was suffering from severe mental strain. I knew, of course, of the "scandal" which was busy with his name and could not but approve of his determination to resign his Chair in the University. He told me that he was shortly taking his wife abroad and would look out for some place in the South or West of France (where they had spent their honeymoon) to settle down in. Within a week, returning from a dinner of one of the University Societies, where he had ceased to be a welcome companion, he found his wife dead upon the divan in their sitting room. At the Inquest he informed the Coroner that he had left her in apparently good health and spirits when he left the house early in the morning. Two days later he was himself taken seriously ill. A virulent form of septic double pneumonia set in almost at once, and in thirty-six hours he was dead. All these tragic happenings formed the almost exclusive topic of conversation in the town and University for a few weeks, and then Magley, his wife and Mrs. Clayton were forgotten. I have pondered deeply whether or not I should destroy this MS. and have more than once been on the point of doing so, but at the critical moment it has seemed to me that I have no right to destroy so astounding a record of research-work in a most obscure field of knowledge. What I think I shall do will be to seal it up again, to be opened long after my death. One thing alone is fortunate, and that is, that neither Paul Barrowdale nor Rex Magley left any ascertainable relations behind them. Barrowdale's fortune reverted, under his Will, to the University; Magley's was escheated to the Crown.

CHRYSTOPHER BLAYRE.

**JASON ROLFE** *An Archive of Human Nonsense*
**ARNAUD RYKNER** *The Last Train*
**LEOPOLD VON SACHER-MASOCH**
  *The Black Gondola and Other Stories*
**MARCEL SCHWOB** *The Assassins and Other Stories*
**MARCEL SCHWOB** *Double Heart*
**CHRISTIAN HEINRICH SPIESS** *The Dwarf of Westerbourg*
**BRIAN STABLEFORD** (editor)
  *Decadence and Symbolism: A Showcase Anthology*
**BRIAN STABLEFORD** (editor) *The Snuggly Satyricon*
**BRIAN STABLEFORD** (editor) *The Snuggly Satanicon*
**BRIAN STABLEFORD** *Spirits of the Vasty Deep*
**COUNT ERIC STENBOCK** *The Shadow of Death*
**COUNT ERIC STENBOCK** *Studies of Death*
**MONTAGUE SUMMERS** *The Bride of Christ and Other Fictions*
**MONTAGUE SUMMERS** *Six Ghost Stories*
**ALICE TÉLOT** *The Inn of Tears*
**GILBERT-AUGUSTIN THIERRY**
  *The Blonde Tress and The Mask*
**DOUGLAS THOMPSON** *The Fallen West*
**TOADHOUSE** *Gone Fishing with Samy Rosenstock*
**TOADHOUSE** *Living and Dying in a Mind Field*
**TOADHOUSE** *What Makes the Wave Break?*
**LÉO TRÉZENIK** *The Confession of a Madman*
**LÉO TRÉZENIK** *Decadent Prose Pieces*
**RUGGERO VASARI** *Raun*
**ILARIE VORONCA** *The Confession of a False Soul*
**ILARIE VORONCA** *The Key to Reality*
**JANE DE LA VAUDÈRE** *The Demi-Sexes and The Androgynes*
**AUGUSTE VILLIERS DE L'ISLE-ADAM** *Isis*
**RENÉE VIVIEN AND HÉLÈNE DE ZUYLEN DE NYEVELT**
  *Faustina and Other Stories*
**RENÉE VIVIEN** *Lilith's Legacy*
**RENÉE VIVIEN** *A Woman Appeared to Me*
**ILARIE VORONCA** *The Confession of a False Soul*
**ILARIE VORONCA** *The Key to Reality*
**TERESA WILMS MONTT** *In the Stillness of Marble*
**TERESA WILMS MONTT** *Sentimental Doubts*
**KAREL VAN DE WOESTIJNE** *The Dying Peasant*